CROAKED IN CALIFORNIA

RAMBLING RV COZY MYSTERIES, BOOK 5

PATTI BENNING

SUMMER PRESCOTT BOOKS PUBLISHING

CHAPTER ONE

"It's bigger than my apartment."

Tulia Blake stared at the hotel room, not realizing she was blocking the doorway until the bellhop cleared his throat behind her. Apologizing, she moved out of his way, but didn't stop staring, at least not until another polite cough made her realize he had finished carrying her things into the room.

"Oh, thank you," she said, setting her purse down on a long table near the entrance and digging her wallet out with one hand. Cicero, her African grey parrot, was perched on her other hand. It had been easier to fold up his travel cage with the other luggage and bring him up to the room in his harness, than to try to wrangle the bulky cage fully assembled through the hallway and elevator.

She handed the bellhop a tip—she wasn't sure how much was appropriate, so she erred on the side of generosity—and waited until he had left the room, shutting the door behind him, to go back to her staring.

She had thought she'd been living in the lap of luxury traveling in her top-of-the-line RV, which cost a good three or four times more than her parents' whole house did, but this hotel made her realize what she'd been missing out on. It wasn't even the most expensive one in San Francisco, and it was still probably the nicest building she had ever been in. She was starting to see why so many lottery winners spent all of their money in just a few years. While she was still determined to beat the odds and make her winnings last her entire life, maybe she should start treating herself just a *little* more often.

The room—well, suite—had high, arched ceilings, and was well lit by the natural light coming in through the wide balcony windows, through which she could see the San Francisco Bay and the Golden Gate Bridge. There were double glass doors that could close off the bedroom, with its four-poster, king-size bed, off of the living room and kitchen area, both of which were bigger than what she'd had in her apartment back in Michigan.

She almost set Cicero down on the back of one of the kitchen chairs that looked like real wood, and quite expensive, then thought better of it and carried him with her as she walked through the hotel suite. The bathroom had two doors, with one entrance in the living room and the other in the bedroom, and when she stepped inside after checking to see if the bed was as soft as it looked, she had to stop and stare again.

The bathroom was all white marble—or some sort of stone, she wasn't an expert—with a huge jacuzzi-style tub in the corner, a separate shower stall, and two sinks. The toilet even had a bidet, along with a small sign explaining how it worked. There was also a generous amount of bathroom products, and they all looked a lot higher quality than the complimentary two-in-one shampoo she was used to seeing at hotels.

"This is it," she said at last as she wandered back into the living room area. "This is paradise. I hope you like San Francisco, buddy, because we're never leaving."

She was joking, mostly. Her self-guided tour around the country was slowly making her realize she might not want to spend her entire life in Michigan, though she loved her home state dearly. She wasn't sure where she wanted to settle down yet. Maybe she would end up living here—but only after she finished her road trip. There was no way she was going to quit partway through, not after what she'd already been through to get this far.

After setting up Cicero's cage first thing and getting him settled in with an early dinner, she started unpacking. Normally, on the rare occasion she stayed at a motel, she lived out of her suitcase, but the dresser and closet in this hotel were so nice it would be a shame not to use them. They even had little scented packets to make her clothes smell nice, which she hadn't known existed until now.

It felt strange to have so much space. She had lived in her RV for the past three and a half months. Now, it was parked in a short-term storage facility on the outskirts of the city, and despite how nice the hotel was, she felt a little homesick for it. It was an easy feeling to push aside, though—she'd be back to it after a week or so, and it was going to be nice to relax and enjoy some of the amenities she could only find in a city. Most of her time on her road trip so far had been spent camping and enjoying the great outdoors, and it was time for a change.

Once she was done unpacking, she went around the hotel room taking some pictures with her phone, then went out onto the balcony with her laptop. She took a few pictures of the view before logging onto her blog. The number of followers she had kept climbing, and she felt obligated to keep things interesting for them. Normally, she kept her exact location vague, but the Golden Gate Bridge was so iconic, she knew her readers would recognize it immediately. She decided to post it anyway; it was a big city, and what were the chances anyone would guess which hotel she was in?

She spent nearly an hour working on her post and then reading through the new comments on her other one. Starting a travel blog hadn't been her idea; a woman named Angela whom she had met in Michigan's Upper Peninsula had suggested it. Angela was her first blog follower, in fact, and commented on almost every post. They chatted through email too, and Tulia thought she might go visit her sometime after she returned to Michigan. She'd met a lot of awesome people on her trip so far, but Angela was the first, and she was glad she counted the woman as a friend now. Plus, she gave good advice; the blog had been a hit, and Tulia had found she really enjoyed updating it. It helped her feel connected on what could have otherwise been a lonely trip.

By the time she was done with the blog, the sun had begun to dip low over the bay, and her stomach was starting to complain. She hadn't eaten since brunch, and it was dinnertime now. She wished Samuel was in town so they could eat together, but he wouldn't be in the area for another day or two. They had lunch plans when he arrived; she'd have to be content eating alone until then.

"Well, time to see if the hotel's restaurant is really as good as the reviews say," she said, rising from the lounge chair on the balcony and carrying her laptop inside. Cicero was contentedly preening on his perch in the cage, and she made kissy noises at him as she set her computer down on the coffee table next to his cage. "You were such a good boy today, buddy. I'm going to go get dinner, but I'll be back soon, okay?"

He'd adjusted to life on the road astonishingly well, and she didn't regret her decision to bring him, even though she occasionally had to adjust her plans around having a pet with her. He was another reason she didn't feel as lonely as she might have otherwise; not many people could say that their pet talked back to them, but Cicero did … when he was in the mood for it. Right now, he just gave her a flat look and tucked his beak into the feathers on his back, preparing for a nap. She got the distinct impression that he wanted her to hurry up and go so he could fall asleep without her chatter.

It felt weird not to double-check that she had her

room key when she stepped into the hallway with her purse looped over her shoulder, but all she needed to access her room was an app on her phone. She paused to make sure her phone wasn't about to die, and while she was checking the status of her battery, the door to the room next to hers opened, and a group of people came out. The sound of giggling made Tulia look up, and she smiled at the sight of the sashes the women were wearing. The one in the center was wearing one that labeled her "Bride-to-Be" and the women on either side of her had sashes that designated them as the "Maid of Honor" and a "Bridesmaid." They were all wearing tight cocktail dresses, and the men were dressed in slacks and button ups. The taller of the two men had his arm around the bride's waist.

They all seemed so happy. Tulia used to think that would be her one day, but then her ex, Luis, cheated on her and ended all the hopes she used to have of marrying him. She still hoped to get married eventually, but right now it was hard to imagine ever being as happy and carefree in a relationship as that bride looked with her groom.

She ended up following the party down the hall to the elevator. Lingering outside when the elevator doors opened, she wasn't sure if she should join them or wait for the next elevator, but the other man, the one who wasn't the groom, held the doors for her and gestured her in.

"Come on," he said. "There's plenty of room."

She stepped into the elevator, and the doors slid shut behind her. "Thanks," she said, offering the man a smile.

"I'm Cody," he said. He seemed a little drunk, or at least buzzed. "You're not part of the bridal party, are you? If you are, you should dance with me at the reception. I bet you'd look pretty in a dress."

Tulia looked at him out of the corner of her eye, not sure if he'd meant that as a compliment or an insult. He'd probably intended it as the former, but she couldn't help feeling slightly offended.

"No, she's not part of the bridal party. They're not arriving until the day after tomorrow," the bride said, rolling her eyes. "Stop flirting, Cody."

"Why? It's not like *I've* got a date to the wedding. I can flirt all I want." One of the other women snorted at that.

The groom stepped forward. "Come on, man, leave her be." He guided his friend away from Tulia, and the bride stepped forward after giving him a quick smile.

"Sorry about that. Cody can be a bit obnoxious when he's been drinking. I'm Callie." She gestured down at herself. "I'm getting married, as you probably guessed. You're in the room next to us, aren't you?"

"Yeah, I am. I'm Tulia. It's nice to meet you. And congratulations."

"Thanks." Callie grinned. "I just wanted to say, if we're too loud, don't hesitate to come knock on our door and tell us to quiet down. The wedding's in four days, but the five of us wanted to spend a few extra days having fun first. Not gonna lie, things might get a bit crazy, but we'll quiet down if it bothers you."

"Don't worry about it," Tulia said, smiling. "I've got a pet bird who can be a little loud sometimes, so I won't complain about any noise I hear from your room if you don't complain about him."

"Deal," Callie said, laughing. "Let me introduce you to Trisha, my maid of honor, and Kasey, my sister. And that's Chase, my fiancé, and that idiot is Cody, his best friend since grade school."

Tulia greeted the others. Trisha, the one who had snorted in response to Cody earlier, was a bit perfunctory, but the others were all friendly enough, and by the time the elevator doors dinged and opened onto the ground floor, she had managed to tell them a bit about her road trip and learned they were going bar hopping for the evening. Callie invited her to come along, but Tulia turned her down, citing her tiredness after a long drive earlier that day.

She almost regretted it as she watched the happy group walk away. She'd been trying to be a lot more outgoing on this trip, really trying to be friendly and connect with strangers. But she just didn't have the energy to go bar hopping tonight. She'd been driving all day, and she was tired. She was looking forward to a good dinner, and then a relaxing evening in her hotel room. If they had asked her tomorrow, it might have been a different story.

"Can I help you, miss?"

She realized she had been staring after the group, and turned her attention to the young man dressed in the hotel's burgundy uniform. His name tag read *Miles, Asst. Manager.* "No, sorry. I was just thinking. Actually, how do I get to the restaurant from here?"

He directed her down the hallway at the far end of the expansive foyer. She thanked him, cast one last look at the bridal party as they exited the hotel, and then went to see what sort of restaurant attached itself to a hotel as nice as this one.

CHAPTER TWO

Tulia returned to her hotel room with a box of
leftovers and a pleasant, warm feeling from the wine
she had imbibed with her dinner of baked scallops.
Cicero woke up as she entered her hotel room, giving
her a quiet "Whatcha doin'?" from his cage. Tulia
spent a moment telling him goodnight and promising
they would do something fun tomorrow, then put her
leftovers in the fridge and retreated to the bedroom.
She dug her pajamas out of the drawer she had stored
them in and went into the bathroom to find out if that
tub was as luxurious as it looked.

She still didn't know what she was going to do
once her trip was over and she returned to Michigan,
or where she was going to live, but she knew wher-
ever she ended up buying a house, she wanted a tub

like this in it. It was almost big enough to be called a hot tub, with a ledge to sit on and jets that soothed her back. She had fun playing around with the tub's various settings before she finally relaxed, leaning back with her head against the edge of the tub while her music played.

She had gotten used to living out of an RV, but she was beginning to miss the comforts of a house or an apartment. A big tub was only one of the things she wished she had; a full-size kitchen was another. And a place to store all her clothes, so she didn't have to leave bags of them in the guest room at her parents' house. She was enjoying her trip, but having an actual home again would be *nice.*

She had possibly the best sleep of her entire life that night, and woke up feeling refreshed and ready to greet the day. She planned on doing activities with Cicero for the first part of the day, and when he was all tuckered out, she would leave him in the hotel room and tour all of the places that weren't bird friendly. There was no rush, though, and she took her time waking up, sitting out on the balcony with her coffee and watching the morning sun gradually light up the San Francisco Bay. She was tempted to call room service for breakfast, but she didn't want to be lazy. She was sure she could find something to eat on the go, and a walking breakfast would be healthier.

Once the coffee worked its magic, she got dressed, got Cicero into his harness, and rode the elevator down to the ground floor. San Francisco was like no city she had ever been to before. Mid Michigan wasn't exactly known for its metropolises, so this was an entirely new experience. She chose a direction at random, deciding to walk along the sidewalk until she spotted something interesting. They were in a touristy area, with local shops and businesses set up nearby to take advantage of the business from the people staying at the luxury hotels with views of the bridge.

It wasn't long before she smelled the delicious scent of fried foods. She followed her nose to a side street lined with food carts. The options seemed endless, and she opted for a breakfast burrito, since it seemed like it would be easy to eat. When she got it, she realized her mistake. It was huge, filled with cheesy scrambled eggs, crisp bacon, fresh tomatoes and onions, and a generous helping of guacamole, all of it topped with a green hot sauce.

Since there was no way she was eating that monstrosity with her hands, she found a bench to sit on so she could attack it with the plastic fork she had been given. She gave Cicero a small piece of the wrap, then dug in. It was good, but a far cry from the healthy breakfast she had envisioned.

She and Cicero spent the rest of the morning walking around the small area of San Francisco they could easily get to by foot from the hotel. She window-shopped, then found a park where they could enjoy a more natural setting for a while. Cicero seemed to be enjoying the fresh air and sunlight, and she took the opportunity to have him stretch his wings, letting him fly from a rock or a tree stump to her while keeping a firm grip on his leash. He was getting more and more confident in the air, and she wondered if she could find some sort of enclosed space where he could fly for longer distances. Maybe a batting cage, if she could find one that was netted in all the way around.

By the time midday came around, she was getting tired of all the walking, and Cicero had settled down on her shoulder, seeming content to just take in the sights. By the time she made it back to the hotel, she was getting hungry again despite the big breakfast, and settled Cicero down in his cage with some fresh fruit to eat before she heated up her leftover dinner from the night before. She munched on it while putting together a new blog post about her morning's sightseeing excursion with Cicero.

When she checked on her bird again, he was taking a nap, his beak tucked beneath the feathers on his back. She gave him a fond smile, quietly shut her laptop, and went into the bedroom to freshen up. Then, she grabbed her phone and her purse and walked out of the suite, making sure the door locked behind her. She took the elevator down to the ground floor, intending to ask a concierge for advice on where to go. San Francisco had seemed like a fun place to stop, and of course she wanted to see the Golden Gate Bridge, but other than that very obvious landmark, she didn't actually know very much about the city. She was excited to learn more.

As she stepped out of the elevator on the ground floor, a woman's raised voice drew her attention to the front desk. The same man who had asked her if he could help her the night before was behind the counter—it was afternoon now, and she figured he probably worked the afternoon and evening shift— talking to a couple of women who Tulia recognized as the women in the room next to hers.

One of the women was talking to Miles, the employee, in a voice that was sharp and high-pitched with anger. Tulia thought her name was Trish or

Trisha, but couldn't remember which. Maybe it was Tracy? Whatever it was, she certainly wasn't happy. Tulia edged closer to the group, not sure if she should get in line. There was a separate concierge desk, but there was no one behind it. Maybe she should just go on her way, but there was a large part of her that was curious as to what had the woman so upset. The bride, Callie, and her sister were standing nearby, both looking irritated as well, though Tulia couldn't tell if their ire was directed toward their companion or the employee.

"I just don't understand how you lost our clothes," Trisha said. Tulia was pretty sure it was Trisha, at least. She really needed to get better at remembering names. "We paid good money to have them washed— a service your hotel advertises as stress-free. You're just lucky none of our outfits for the wedding were in there. What are we supposed to wear until then, though? Do you understand how much some of our clothing costs?"

"Miss, I assure you, your clothing will be returned to you. All I said was I didn't have your order on my docket for today. We haven't lost anything. We'll have them for you by this evening, I'll make sure of it myself."

"Well, you'd better," Trisha said. "We're going to

be leaving a very bad review. We expected much better service from a hotel that's this expensive. And you'd better believe I'll be complaining to your boss. This is unacceptable."

With that, she spun on her heel, turning to rejoin the other two women. Callie's sister shot Trisha a look full of disapproval but Callie just sighed.

"Let's go, Trisha. We're going to be late to get our nails done," Callie said.

"I might stay here. I really need to talk to Chase about something," Trisha said, looking uncomfortable.

"What could you possibly want with my fiancé?" Callie asked, sounding amused.

Trisha pressed her lips together. "It's about the wedding."

"If he's got something up his sleeve, he and Cody can handle it. You're coming with us; I booked the appointment for the three of us, and if you don't go now, they won't be able to get you in la—" Callie turned and saw Tulia standing not far behind her. She broke off, clapped a hand to her lips in surprise, then gave a forced laugh. "Oh. It's you. Sorry, you startled me."

"Sorry, I didn't mean to," Tulia said. "I was just going to…" She gestured awkwardly toward the front desk, where Miles was frantically typing on his computer.

"Oh, of course," Callie said, stepping aside to let Tulia by.

Trisha sniffed loudly as she walked past and said, "If you need anything important, I wouldn't use any of the services the hotel offers. I learned the hard way that they can't be trusted."

"Trisha, just drop it already," the third member of the bridal party, Kasey said. "We'll find our laundry. It's not his fault that it got lost. Can we just go? Come on, I want to get coffee first."

They left, Callie waving goodbye to Tulia while the other two argued back and forth. Feeling bad for the man behind the counter, she gave him her most pleasant smile, perfected after years of waitressing.

"Hi, Miles, right?" she asked, reading his name tag again. He looked up from the computer, giving her a tight smile in return.

"Yes. Sorry about your wait, we had an issue with our laundry service. How can I help you?"

"I was just wondering if you have some suggestions of fun things to do in the area? I've never been to San Francisco before, and I'm not sure where to begin."

"Unfortunately, our concierge went home for the

day, but I've lived here my whole life. I'm happy to give you some suggestions. If you give me just a second, I can write up a list for you?"

She thanked him and didn't have to wait long until he handed her a neatly printed list full of ideas of things to do. She thanked him, and he looked a little bit more relaxed as he told her to enjoy her day.

She promised she would, and as she left the hotel, she tried to push the argument out of her mind. She just hoped he enjoyed his day too. No one deserved to be treated like that. After that display, she no longer regretted not going out for drinks the night before.

.

CHAPTER THREE

She returned that evening exhausted, but in a good
way. She'd eaten while she was out, but when she got
up to her room, she ordered a drink from room
service. She normally didn't drink much, since she
wanted to be able to drive her RV if she ever needed
to move it. But now that she was living without her
wheels for a while, there was no reason not to have a
glass of wine before bed.

She let Cicero sit on the back of the armchair, a
towel underneath him so he didn't damage it, while
she flipped through channels on the television. It had
been a long time since she watched anything on live
TV, and it was weird having advertisements interrupt
every few minutes again. She was just about to give

up and stream something on her laptop when someone knocked on the door.

A man called out, "Room service," and she opened the door to find Miles standing there with her drink. She thanked him, took the wine, and had to duck back inside for a tip.

When she handed it to him, she said, "I'm surprised they have a manager delivering room service."

He shook his head, a faint expression of irritation crossing his face. "This isn't normally my job, but we are very short-staffed right now. Well, I say right now, but we've been short-staffed for a while."

"I hope things get better soon," Tulia said. "The restaurant I used to waitress at never hired enough people. I think the owners didn't understand how much smoother everything would've gone with just a few more employees."

"Well, the hotel's website does have an anonymous review feature," he said. He winked, then added, "Just in case you want to give my boss any tips."

Laughing, she let him get back to his job, shutting the door and returning to the comfortable armchair with her wine. She had left the TV on a random channel when she walked away, and now it was showing a nature documentary about ocean fish. It wasn't the most engrossing thing, but Cicero seemed intrigued by it. Since nothing else had really caught her interest, she decided to leave it on.

She was almost done with her glass of wine and was beginning to feel drowsy when she heard a loud thump from the neighboring wall. She jumped slightly and put the wine down on the coffee table, turning to stare at the wall. That was the side the bridal party was on, and she wondered what they were getting up to in there. She would have expected to hear music, or maybe loud voices, not this.

It was just one thump, though, and was hardly something to complain about. She turned her attention back to the TV but didn't have time to pick up her wine again before she heard another thump. This one was louder, as if someone had thrown something heavy at the wall. She stared at the wall again, and was beginning to wonder if everything was okay, but she didn't hear any more sounds. Maybe they were rearranging the furniture? That seemed likely, especially if they had a party planned.

She watched the show for another few minutes, sipping the last of her wine and carefully taking the glass over to the small sink in the dedicated kitchen area, where room service would pick it up the next day. Cicero was asleep on the back of the chair. If it had been her apartment, she might have let him sleep out of his cage for the night, but she didn't want to chance it in such an unfamiliar room. Waking him up quietly, she carried him back over to his cage, kissed his black beak, and let him step onto his favorite sleeping perch. She whispered good night to him and turned out the lights.

She took two steps toward the bedroom, where the soft glow of the bedside table's lamp was lighting her way, when a woman screamed—a horrible, devastated sound. Cicero responded with a shocked flutter of his wings and a squawk, and Tulia nearly jumped out of her skin. The sound had come from the neighboring room. She turned the lights back on. There was a raised voice coming from the other side of the wall, and as she moved closer, she heard quiet sobbing through the wall as well.

She had gone from amused and curious to frightened and concerned. Had someone been injured? Had something precious been broken? She hesitated, but the sobs weren't dying off. If anything, they were getting louder. Worried, she put her shoes on, grabbed her phone, and stepped out of the hotel room.

She walked across to the other door and knocked on it. After a long wait, someone depressed the handle and pulled the door open. It was Callie, the bride, but she was almost unrecognizable. Her eyes were puffy and red, her eye makeup was smeared, and her cheeks were wet with tears.

"I can't believe it," she said, her voice breaking as she stared at Tulia. "I didn't want to believe it. Maybe I'm wrong. Maybe Kasey and I are both wrong. Can you come check?"

"Come check what?" Tulia asked, part of her already wanting to recoil from the woman and whatever was in that room.

"It's Trisha," Callie said, her hand shaking as she used it to wipe her tears. "I think she's dead."

Tulia did not want to help. She didn't want to check to see if a woman was dead. She didn't want to be involved in this. She wanted to return to her hotel room, turn the TV up, and pretend none of this had ever happened.

But Callie was crying, and she remembered the thudding, the sounds she had ignored. Guilt twisted in her. She nodded. "Let me see."

Callie moved back, pulling the door open, and Tulia stepped inside. The room was a mess, but the sort of mess that came from people who had stuffed their suitcases too full for their vacation. Wedding decorations, articles of clothing, and various haircare and makeup products were strewn across the suite. The air in the room smelled strongly of perfume, and she could hear music coming faintly from the bedroom. The couch was a pullout—hers must be too, she hadn't checked—and the bedding on it was rumpled and half-made.

She took all of that in in a second, because the two people near the far wall drew her attention. One of them, Kasey, was sitting with her back against the wall, her arms wrapped around her knees, staring blankly at the woman in front of her.

The woman on the ground was Trisha. Her pretty hair was mussed, and her eyes were open and staring at the ceiling. There was a bloodstain on the carpet under her head, and a matching red smudge on the corner of the long table against the wall a few feet away.

Tulia stared at her. There was no question she was dead, but Callie pushed her toward the woman. "Can you try checking, please? We took her pulse, and we couldn't find anything, and Kasey tried CPR, but nothing is working. I don't know what to do."

Tulia stumbled forward in a daze, kneeling next to the woman and inexpertly taking her pulse. The feel of the woman's skin beneath her fingers was all wrong. She felt her wrist, trying to remember the lessons she learned in health class, but that was years ago. She felt nothing, no beat beneath her fingers or flex of the other woman's muscles. Trisha was still staring blankly at the ceiling. A piece of lint was on her eye, and she wasn't blinking it away.

"She's dead." Her voice sounded strange and blank to her, and behind her, Callie started sobbing again. Kasey looked up at her, a determined expression coming into her eyes.

"We have to call the police. Someone did this to her. Someone murdered her."

CHAPTER FOUR

Tulia wasn't the one who called the police. Kasey took that upon herself, suddenly seeming to come to her senses. She ordered the other two women back from the body, and Tulia stood in the corner, not sure what to do or say while Callie sat on the unmade pullout bed and cried. Kasey dialed the emergency number on her phone and explained the situation to the dispatcher in as clear a way as she could, though she had to stop occasionally to keep from breaking down in tears. Finally, Kasey hung up the phone and let it fall onto the pullout bed next to Callie. She stared at Trisha on the floor. Tulia didn't want her to do that the whole time they waited for the first responders to arrive, so she cleared her throat.

"What happened? I heard some thudding, but I didn't think…" She trailed off.

"I don't know," Kasey whispered. "Callie and I, we were both out of the room. I was trying to handle the laundry issues, she was at the gym. We… We didn't think we should leave Trisha to do it, since she was so upset earlier. When I got back, the room door was ajar, and I found her like this. Someone killed her. Who would do that? It had to be someone who works here, right? How else would they get into the room?"

"I don't know," Tulia said. She kept glancing at the body, then looking away. It was like her eyes were being drawn to it against her will. "The police will figure it out. It's their job."

She was sure there were plenty of security cameras in a hotel like this. With luck, it would be an open and shut case, and whoever had killed Trisha would be behind bars in a matter of hours.

When the police arrived, they ushered the women out of the room. They questioned them in the hallway at first, then in Tulia's room after she offered it up for their use. She carried Cicero's cage into her bedroom and shut the door so he wouldn't be disturbed, and then seated herself on the couch, listening to the chaotic rush of voices as the emergency responders took stock of the situation.

When questioned, she told them about the sounds she heard, and gave her best guess as to what time it had been. The questions made her throat thicken with another surge of guilt. She should have checked on them. She had thought they were just being loud. She had thought they were having fun.

The whole affair took hours. By the time the police left, Trisha's body already gone with the coroner and crime scene tape hung across the door, the hotel staff had managed to wrangle some higher-ups, who were doing their best to mitigate the problems involved in the situation. They were determined to move everyone in the hall to different rooms, but they didn't have enough open ones.

Some people got vouchers for free stays at neighboring hotels, but Tulia, Trisha, Callie, and when they got back after their late night out, Chase and Cody, all got offered rooms in another part of the hotel. Tulia accepted because, by now, she was exhausted, and she didn't want to move all her stuff to another hotel at midnight.

The staff moved her things to her new room, and she did nothing but cling to Cicero's cage as the employees got her settled into it. This one didn't have a view of the bridge and the bay, and one of the staff members was swearing up and down that they would refund her for a portion of her stay, but she barely heard them. She spotted Callie and Kasey going into the room beside her. Chase and Cody had a room across the hall, but as soon as the staff left, Chase went to embrace his fiancée. Tulia left them to it. She didn't want to talk. She just wanted to be alone.

Slipping into her new room, she deadbolted the door behind her, then double checked that no one was hiding in any of the closets or under the bed. Trisha's death had spooked her, and she didn't feel quite as secure in the hotel anymore. With Cicero's cage on top of the dresser in her bedroom and her suitcase still unpacked on the floor, she climbed into bed and lay in the dark, staring up at the ceiling.

She should have been tired. She should have been exhausted—and she was. She was so tired she could barely think straight, but part of her brain was wide awake, wondering what happened, going over everything again and again. She didn't know what she was going to do tomorrow, whether she was going to stay or go. Maybe she should get another hotel across the city. This one felt more like a prison than a place to relax now.

She tried not to think about the way Trisha had

lain there on the floor, so still. She tried not to think about the sounds of the attack she had heard and ignored. She tried, but she failed, because all she could think of was the murder and the mystery of who had done it, and why.

CHAPTER FIVE

She slept terribly, tossing and turning until the sky was turning gray with the morning's light. Then, she finally managed to drift off into a restful sleep. When she woke up, it was already late morning, and she had a slew of notifications on her phone. Most were about comments on her blog, but she'd missed a call from her mother and a text message from Samuel. She checked the text first. *I'm just getting to town. Have you had a chance to scope out any good restaurants? Where do you want to meet?*

With a jolt of panic, she realized today was the day she was supposed to meet Samuel for lunch. She had forgotten about it in the chaos of the night before. She sent a quick text back to him, saying, *The hotel restaurant is pretty good, or if you want something else, I can ask around. What are you in the mood for?*

He had only sent the message half an hour ago, so at least he hadn't been waiting too long for a reply. She wasn't going to tell him she had just woken up. She didn't even remember the last time she had slept this late, and everything felt out of place.

She quickly got dressed, a lightheaded feeling telling her she couldn't wait until they met to eat something. She started the coffee maker, took Cicero out of his cage and let him stand on the back of a chair again, and started chopping up a banana and an apple she'd picked up on her last shopping trip for him. Both were beginning to show their age, but he never seemed to care. Once the coffee was done, she sat down at the small table, gave Cicero his bowl of fruit, and looked over the room service menu, hoping to find something light and healthy to tide her over until she and Samuel met.

Her phone buzzed. *I'm happy to meet at the hotel. Stopped to get gas. I think I could be there in an hour. Which one are you staying at again?*

She texted him the name of the hotel, promised to meet him at the restaurant for lunch, then returned to pouring over the room service menu. She just wanted a cup of fruit or something similar. She could eat one of Cicero's bananas, but they were going a bit brown, and while he liked them mushy, she definitely didn't.

Before she could make her choice, she spotted the fine print at the bottom of the menu telling her room service could take as long an hour to an hour and a half to arrive. By then, she'd already be meeting with Samuel. She decided to head down and grab something from the complimentary breakfast the hotel offered … assuming it was still open.

She put Cicero back in his cage with his own breakfast, his "See you later," as she left making her feel bad for leaving him on his own, and set off down the hall, shooting a glance toward the door belonging to Callie and Kasey's room.

Had they left? She couldn't imagine that the wedding was going ahead, not after what happened. Or maybe they were sticking around in hopes that they would find out what happened to their friend.

Moving quickly, she took the elevator down to the ground floor and looked around for the complimentary breakfast area. There was a small sign by the front desk pointing the way and as she turned down the hallway it guided her toward, she saw a pair of police officers talking to a man with a name tag that told her he was the hotel's manager. She slowed her pace as she walked, trying not to call attention to herself even though she was bursting with curiosity.

"I don't know what happened," the manager was saying. "I wasn't even here last night. My assistant manager isn't answering my texts or my calls, but I can tell you he didn't have access to the cameras. Only the security team has access to them, and you already questioned them."

"Sir, six hours of security footage went missing. Someone knows what happened to it. We've spoken to everyone who was on the shift roster for last night, and they all denied knowing anything. Would anyone have been working who isn't on the roster?"

"No, we are all supposed to log in under our own code, and the hours are tracked under each person's name. None of my employees did this. I'm telling you, it has to have been someone who came in from outside or a guest."

By then, Tulia was getting too far past them to continue eavesdropping. If she went any slower, the officers were going to notice she was stalling. Still, what she had managed to overhear had given her a lot to think about. The security footage was missing. That seemed to fit with Kasey's theory that an employee had done it, but why? Why kill Trisha, of all people? What motive could they possibly have had?

She thought of Trisha's argument with Miles and frowned. Trisha had been beyond rude to him, but it seemed like a stretch to call that a motive for murder.

She shook her head, trying to ignore the temptation to investigate further. She needed food, then she needed to finish getting ready for her date. Or whatever it was. There was definitely something there between her and Samuel, but they hadn't talked about it. Maybe they should. He had delayed going back home and now was extending his vacation to hit a lot of the same stops she was. That had to mean something.

She wouldn't deny that she liked him. He was interesting, shared her love of solving mysteries, handsome, and seemed a lot more responsible than Luis was. Still, she barely knew him. The experiences they had gone through together had been intense, which was probably why she felt as close to him as she did, but at the end of the day, he was still almost a stranger to her. This date would be the start of something more, of getting to know who he was when he wasn't working a case or tracking down a killer.

At the breakfast bar, she grabbed a small container of yogurt and a small bowl of cereal before she went back upstairs. The manager and the police officers were gone, and anyone who was just arriving would have no indication that the hotel had seen a brutal murder the night before.

Back in her hotel room, she mixed the yogurt and cereal together for a quick breakfast, then did her hair and makeup, taking a little more time than she usually did. By the time she was finished, her hour was nearly up. She was putting on her shoes when Samuel texted her.

Just pulled in. Where should I meet you?

Smiling, she finished slipping her shoes on and texted back, *I'll come down. See you soon.*

CHAPTER SIX

She met him just inside the doors to the hotel. She waved as she approached and stopped a few feet away from him, not sure if they should hug in greeting or not. It had been a while since they'd seen each other, having gone their separate ways to explore different parts of California.

For a second, he looked like he was about to hug her, and she was beginning to raise her arms when he seemed to change his mind, changing the motion into holding his hand out to shake. Flustered, she shook his hand and then gestured toward where the restaurant was.

"Shall we? I think they just opened, so it should be easy to get a table."

"Lead the way," he said, looking around. "Man, I travel a lot for my job, but I don't think I've ever been in a hotel this nice. I'll have to talk to the agency about that. I guess it doesn't exactly have the whole detective noir thing going on, but I'd be willing to sacrifice some atmosphere for a lack of mysterious stains and clean sheets."

She laughed. "I still feel like an imposter here, to be honest. I've been in my fair share of shady motels too, and I hate to say it, but I just don't think I can go back." For a second she considered telling him about the plush bed and the amazing bath, but realized that might be taken the wrong way. Instead, she said, "My first room had a great view of the bridge and the bay. My other one just looks out onto the road, but it's still not too bad. San Francisco is a pretty city."

"Why did you have to change rooms?" he asked as they walked into the restaurant area. Tulia grimaced. She hadn't wanted to start with this.

"I'll tell you in a second," she promised as the hostess greeted them. They were seated at a small, two-person table. Their waiter left them with their menus, and she perused the lunch section, which she had skipped over the last time she'd eaten there. The scallops had been delicious, but she wasn't in the mood for seafood right now. Chicken sounded good. The Caesar salad chicken wraps sounded perfect; she must not have been eating enough fruits and vegetables, because the side of steamed broccoli and seasonal fruit sounded amazing. She was definitely going to have to work on having a better diet; when money wasn't a concern, it was too easy to eat out all the time.

Once they had placed their orders, Samuel opting for chicken as well, though he got the chicken parmesan pasta, he arched an eyebrow at her. "So, why did you have to switch rooms?"

She bit her lip. As much as Samuel shared her love of mysteries, it was a job to him. He solved the mysteries he was hired to solve, and if they were too dangerous or too intense for him, he didn't have any qualms about telling the client he couldn't help them. Chasing down the serial killer they had caught in Montana had been an exception. It had become a personal case for him, and solving it had almost killed him.

To her, all of the mysteries she'd gotten involved in over these past few months were personal. This one felt even more personal somehow, since she had heard the murder while it was happening. She wanted to at least stick around until they had some answers, but she knew he wouldn't agree with that choice. As far as he was concerned, there was no good reason for her to risk life and limb trying to solve a mystery that the local police department had well in hand. And even worse, he had a point. But she wasn't going to lie to him. She had brought it up, and now she had to follow through and tell him the full story.

"So, remember how you were talking about there being a curse on my RV the other day, when that guy tried to steal my catalytic converter at the gas station?"

He nodded slowly. "Considering how many times you've almost been murdered in that vehicle, had it stolen, or parts of it stolen, I stand by what I said. That thing is cursed."

"Well, you might want to rethink that. If there *is* a curse, I'm pretty sure it's on me, not the RV. I left it in a lot across the city, but the curse struck again." She gave a weak laugh, but he wasn't fooled.

"Are you okay? Did someone get hurt?"

"Someone died," she admitted, her voice dropping and all humor vanishing from it. "A woman who was in the room next to mine. She was killed last night, and no one knows how or why."

A pained expression came across his face. "You

feel somehow obligated to look into it, don't you?" She nodded, wincing and expecting him to argue against it, but he just sighed. "It's not my place to tell you what to do. I'm sure whatever happened, it must've been horrible. I'm just worried you're going to get hurt."

"I'll be careful," she said. "I'm not going to try to play detective, I just want to stick around for a little while and see what's going on. Just this morning, I overheard the police talking to the manager. The security footage from last night is all missing. It sounds like it was deleted. Someone is definitely trying to cover this up."

"Tell you what," he said. "I'll stick around, get a hotel in the area—" He broke off, looking around at the restaurant. "Maybe not somewhere quite so nice. If you give me a list of names, I'll run background checks on them. It won't be anything the police can't do, but it might answer some of your questions."

She was surprised, and wondered if he was only making this offer out of the hope that it would keep her from getting personally involved by questioning the people she thought might be possible suspects. "Thanks. I think I'll take you up on that."

She'd given him most of the details of what had happened by the time their food came. Her wrap looked delicious, and tasted just as good as it looked. Their conversation paused while they started eating, and when it picked up again, they spent some time catching up on everything else they had each done since they last saw each other. It felt nice, comparing notes about all the things they'd done. Knowing that she'd see him again in a few days or weeks was comforting. She might be across the country from her family and friends, but she wasn't alone.

Finally, the conversation came back around to her, and he asked her about her ex. Normally, this might have been a red flag in a potential new boyfriend, but she'd told him all about Luis a long time ago. Samuel had been helping her figure out how to keep the private investigator Luis had hired from pestering her family.

"I tried calling the agency myself," he told her. "I got the same response you did. Without a formal police report of harassment or proof of illegal activity, they aren't going to cancel their contract with him."

"They haven't bothered my parents again, at least," Tulia said, sighing. "I'm on the other side of the country from Luis. As long as he isn't sending anyone to bother my family, I guess he can keep looking for me. And I'll admit, it is the tiniest bit satisfying knowing he's throwing all of his money away searching for me. Even if he finds me, he's not getting a dime."

"You're across the country from him for now," Samuel said. "You won't be forever, unless you're planning on staying out here. I'm worried about your safety when you return to Michigan."

"You shouldn't be," she said. "I don't think Luis would actually hurt me." She hesitated. "Do you?"

"I don't know him," Samuel said. "But I have seen people driven to do things they normally wouldn't when money is on the line." He lowered his voice. "Considering the amount of money you have, people will kill over that, Tulia. Be careful, okay? Money and greed can change people. Even if the Luis you knew wouldn't hurt you, this Luis, the one who thinks you owe him a million bucks? He is not the same guy."

Tulia shifted uncomfortably, stabbing her fork through a couple of pieces of seasoned broccoli. The food was good, and she was glad she'd ordered it, but the warning tone in Samuel's voice made her stomach turn sour.

"I hate this. I wish he had never found out about the stupid lottery ticket."

"I'll keep trying to think of ways to help you,"

Samuel said. "I'm sorry you have to deal with this. It can't be fun."

"No, it isn't," she said. "But at least he's there and I'm here. For now, I don't have to worry about it."

Though having an actual murderer to worry about wasn't much better.

CHAPTER SEVEN

After dinner, she and Samuel went to one of the local bars for a drink, then walked outside for a while, looking at the San Francisco Bay and enjoying the very alive feel of the city around them. After that, they went their separate ways. He was staying at a hotel in the area, though not as pricey as hers. It was nice, having someone to share her trip with in this way. As much as she was enjoying herself, she couldn't deny that it was lonely, which was one of the reasons she had started her blog. Even though she didn't know most of the people who followed it, there was still a sense of camaraderie.

Thinking about her blog made her realize she should update it before she went to bed. When she returned to her room, she said hello to Cicero and then sat at the suite's table with her laptop, ready to get to work.

She wasn't going to mention the murder. Maybe she would at some point, but she had a policy of never updating the blog with any details about an ongoing police investigation. She didn't want to take the chance of wrecking the work the police had done on the case.

Keeping it vague, she just mentioned that something had happened in the hotel, and they had moved her to a different room. She took a quick picture of the room and uploaded it, glad that she hadn't made a mess of it yet. Then, she focused on the rest of her day, telling her readers she had met up with "a friend" and they'd enjoyed a nice dinner together. She took a picture of Cicero perched contentedly on the back of one of the chairs, proofread the whole thing, and posted it. It wasn't her most exciting update, but at the end of the day, she was doing this blog for herself, not for anyone else. If her readers didn't like the occasional boring update, well, they didn't have to read it.

By then it was getting late, but she wasn't tired quite yet. She felt energized despite her walk, or maybe because of it. It was a good reminder that exercise was good for her and she should probably do it more. She wasn't spending all day on her feet waiting tables anymore; spending the day behind the wheel of her RV didn't exactly burn calories or count toward cardio.

Even though she wasn't ready for bed yet, she couldn't think of anything else she wanted to do. None of the shows she usually kept up with sounded appealing right now, and she wasn't sure she wanted to read a book either. She felt ... uninspired. Bored.

She logged onto her social media account, something she hadn't been doing as much lately. She didn't want her friends and her extended family members to know about her lottery winnings, but there wasn't a good way to explain her trip without revealing the truth. Her blog was somewhat anonymous, in that she didn't use her real name, and she didn't post full pictures of herself. So far, that had been good enough to keep most people from finding out about her lottery winnings. Luis was an exception, and she supposed she owed him her thanks for not spreading the truth around when he found out how she was able to afford her trip.

She had a bunch of notifications to read through, mostly things like birthdays she had missed and people tagging her in photos and memes. She responded to a few, then resorted to the soothing, strangely addictive action of scrolling, reading post after post but not really taking any of them in.

It was strange, how little had changed in her friend group back home. One of the waitresses she used to be friends with at the restaurant she had worked at before winning the lottery had quit, and another of her friends was announcing an engagement, but overall for most of them, it was life as usual. If she hadn't won the lottery, she wondered what she would be doing right now. She would probably still be working the same job, which hadn't been horrible, but it hadn't exactly been taking her anywhere either. Maybe she would have started dating again, but probably not. Either way, she knew there was no version of her that would have gotten back together with Luis.

Her computer dinged to alert her as a message came in. It was from one of her friends, Leslie, an ex-coworker who she had kept in touch with. She and Luis had gone on some double dates with Leslie and her boyfriend, Aaron, and this time a year ago, she would have said they were all friends.

Hey, I just saw that you were online, and I wanted to say hi. I haven't heard much from you since the breakup. How are you doing?

Knowing she had been a bad friend to pretty much

everyone she knew since she took off out of Michigan without a word to any of them, she typed back, *I'm doing great. Just been really busy lately, sorry. How are you?*

The reply came only seconds later. *I'm good! Aaron and I split up, but it was mutual, nothing dramatic like what happened with you and Luis. I was so mad when I heard. I'm glad you got the word out, because he definitely tried to blame the breakup on you.*

Tulia pressed her lips together. A couple days after her breakup with Luis, after the first huge shock of winning the lottery had subsided slightly, she made a post detailing their breakup, still hurt and eager to try to make him suffer as much as she had. She wasn't surprised to learn he had tried to spin things so he looked good.

I'm just glad he showed his true colors sooner rather than later, she typed back. *I'll really be happy if I never see him again. Is he still hanging out with you guys a lot?* She was going to return to Michigan eventually, and she really didn't want to have to worry about coming face-to-face with him when she got back together with her old friend group.

She waited while Leslie typed. *Not with me, but I*

know he hung out with the guys once or twice. I haven't heard anything since he left, though.

The words sent an icy chill through her as she read them. With a creeping certainty, she typed, *What do you mean, he left? When? Where did he go?*

Geez, girl, I thought you said you were over him, her friend replied with a laughing emoji.

I am. This is serious. Did he leave the state?

I'm not sure. Aaron mentioned it in passing. He mentioned Luis had taken off for his "Great American Road Trip", and we joked about how he probably wouldn't get farther than the next county, since his car breaks down every two seconds.

Tulia's heart was beating so hard in her chest she wondered if she was in danger of having a heart attack. Just hours ago, she had told Samuel she didn't think Luis would actually hurt her, but as it turned out, she didn't believe her own words. The thought of him finding her was terrifying.

When did he leave? she asked, her hands shaking.

Last week, or the week before, I'd have to ask Aaron, Leslie responded. *Is everything all right?*

Everything's fine, Tulia said. *I've got to go.*

She exited out of the browser and shut her laptop without waiting for a response. She would have to apologize to Leslie later, but right now she felt as if she couldn't breathe. A week, maybe two. More than enough time for him to drive across the country.

The air in the room felt cloying, and she took a deep, jagged breath as she stumbled toward the balcony door, throwing it open and stepping outside. The motion sensitive light turned on, illuminating the balcony for her. She inhaled deeply, letting the sounds of the city wash over her as she slowly sank down, her back against the slats of the balcony as she looked out and down at the ground thirty feet below. Forcing herself to breathe deeply and slowly, she tried not to think about Luis, or anything at all.

CHAPTER EIGHT

Slowly, Tulia began to feel better, the cool night air soothing against her skin. Still sitting, she looked up at the stars, past the balcony above her. The light had turned off after she was still for a few minutes, but she still couldn't see much of the night sky. She wished she was camping somewhere remote so she could see them sparkle across the entire sky instead of just the measly one or two that poked through the city lights.

It had been stupid of her, so stupid, to post her location in the blog. She should have waited until after she left the area to post about it. Sure, she never gave street or business names, but it would still be easy for someone determined, someone like Luis, to find her. Now, he knew where she was. For all she knew, he was waiting outside her hotel room door this very second. All of her certainty when she was talking with Samuel earlier must have had more to do with the distance between them than faith that he wouldn't hurt her. Right now, if she ran into him in a dark alley, she would be afraid for her life.

She took a deep breath again, trying to think about the situation logically. Even if he figured out which hotel she was in, he wouldn't know which room was hers, and that was assuming he had even made it across the country to begin with. While Leslie had been joking about the condition of his car, it was a joke rooted in truth. The thing seemed to break down every other day. She wasn't sure how Luis was funding his trip, or how he had been affording the private investigators for that matter, or the time off work. However he was getting the money for it, she knew he must be desperate. Desperate people were the most dangerous.

She knew she should call Samuel, let him know what was going on. Maybe he'd even come and spend the night in her suite, making use of the pull-out couch. With him around, she would feel safe. Then in the morning, she could check out and head somewhere else, somewhere unexpected. Somewhere Luis wouldn't think to look for her.

She was about to get up and put her plan into motion when she heard the neighboring balcony door slide open. Two people, a man and a woman, came out, shutting the door behind them.

"We can't keep doing this," the man said, his voice low and furtive. "It doesn't feel right."

"No one is going to find out." That was the woman. Tulia couldn't tell whether it was Callie or Kasey, but she was certain it had to be one of them. That was their room, after all.

"That doesn't change the way I feel." There was silence for a moment, then the man said, "Do you think the wedding is off?"

"I don't know," the woman said. "What happened to Trisha…"

"Someone died," the man said. "It's a good reason to call off the wedding. For good, even."

Tulia heard a sigh and began quietly getting to her feet, intending to try to get a look at the people who were talking.

Above her head, the motion sensitive light went on. She had completely forgotten about it. She heard a gasp, and the other balcony door slid open again. By the time she got to her feet, the two people were gone.

Tulia glared at the light that had wrecked her attempts to spy, then went inside herself. She wasn't sure what to make of what she had overheard. It seemed like a normal conversation about the wedding, but if that was the case, why were the two people being so furtive?

She was curious and couldn't shake the sense that something was going on with the wedding party. Thinking about the mystery was a great distraction from Luis. It was also a good reminder that she was on the third floor of a nice hotel, with the door securely locked between her and the rest of the world. That maybe wasn't quite as comforting as it would have been before Trisha's death, but she knew there was no way Luis could get to her right now. There was no need to disturb Samuel tonight or try to get him to come all the way from his hotel just to keep her company. She would be safe here, and in the morning, she could pack up her things and leave without causing a scene.

She had left Cicero out in her panic, and as soon as she came in, he leapt off the chair, flapping over to her. She caught him on her hand, smiling despite everything. "Good job. That's what I like to see. You're using those wings of yours."

She kissed him on the beak and put him in his cage, partially covering it with a blanket. That would give him some dark space to sleep while she was still up with the lights on, but if he felt lonely, he could watch her from the uncovered side.

She sat at the table with her laptop again, but this time intending to see if she could unblock Luis and see any updates on his social media accounts. Maybe he had posted about where he was going, or kept track of his trip in some other way. She might be able to sneak a look before he realized what she was doing.

She had just opened her laptop when she heard a sharp knock on her hotel door. She froze, listening to see if it would come again.

It did. Taking in a shaky breath, she stood up and slowly, quietly, walked over to the door, standing on her tiptoes to look through the peephole.

When she saw Kasey standing in the hall, relief washed through her. She undid the deadbolt and opened the door.

"Hey, what's going on?"

"I saw the light on underneath the door, and came to see how you're doing," Kasey said. "What happened with … with Trisha." She paused to take a deep breath, closing her eyes. "Sorry, we're still in shock about it. I wanted to apologize for dragging you into it like we did. Callie and I, neither of us have ever dealt with anything like this before. It wasn't fair for us to bring you into that. Now, you're tied up in all of this too. You even had to move rooms because of us."

"I would've had to move rooms anyway," she pointed out. "The hotel staff moved everyone out of that hall. Either way, you shouldn't feel bad for asking for help."

"Well, we appreciate it," Kasey said. She looked past Tulia's shoulder and into her room, "Are you sure you're doing all right? You're all alone in there."

"I'll be fine," Tulia said. "A bit jumpy, but that's to be expected."

"Yeah." Kasey gave a weak smile. "I've definitely been a lot more paranoid today. I keep jumping at every sound, and I have to keep reminding myself her killer probably isn't about to jump out of the bathroom cabinet in the middle of my shower."

"I know what you mean," Tulia said. "It's hard not to be afraid, but I keep reminding myself I'm on the third floor, I've looked in every nook and cranny in here, and no one can get in with the deadbolt turned. I'll be okay. Thanks for checking in, though."

"Just let us know if you need anything. If you want to join us or whatever, feel free to. We're going to turn in for the night soon, but we'll probably be up for a while, watching TV."

"Thanks, I'll keep that in mind."

Kasey left, and she shut the door, making sure to turn the deadbolt, wondering. Was Kasey's visit a coincidence, or was she trying to figure out if Tulia had overheard the conversation on the balcony?

She shook her head, turning back to the couch. She was just feeding into the paranoia now. Nothing in the short conversation she had overheard was incriminating by itself. Trisha's death was making them all paranoid. She had to remind herself it wasn't her concern. She had enough to worry about with Luis.

CHAPTER NINE

When she woke up the next morning, Tulia decided she was being an idiot. Samuel had offered her his help again and again. By keeping the news about Luis leaving Michigan from him, she wasn't doing either of them a favor. She was just putting herself in more danger, and she was keeping him in the dark for no reason other than her own pride and the desire not to worry him.

She felt a lot better with the morning sunlight streaming in through the windows, the lively sounds of traffic, both pedestrian and vehicular, coming from the street below, and the smell of coffee permeating the air. She put Cicero in his harness, and the two of them sat out on the balcony, enjoying the morning air. The knowledge that Luis could be nearby wasn't as frightening, not when she was up this high. She felt in control. Before that feeling faded, she sent a quick text message out to Samuel.

Hey, can we get together again today? She named the park she had gone to a couple of days ago with Cicero. By the time she had gone back inside and thrown her coffee cup away in the kitchen trash, he had responded.

20 minutes?

She smiled and typed out a quick response. *Make it 30.* She still had to get dressed and do her hair and makeup, but if she hurried, she should make it there just in the nick of time.

Walking the streets of San Francisco with Cicero on her shoulder and the morning still fresh around her made her glad she had decided to spend time in the city, despite everything that had happened. It was a completely different world than the one she had grown up in. She wasn't sure she would want to live in a large city like this for the rest of her life, but for a year or two? She thought it would be fun, especially once she got all of the troubles with Luis figured out. The day he stopped harassing her, she was sure she would feel a huge weight lift off her back.

Once she got to the park, she texted Samuel, and they managed to find each other. He said hello to

Cicero first, and the bird responded with a low whistle. When he turned his attention to her, she was already smiling. Luis had never paid any attention to Cicero, other than to tell him to be quiet.

"So, is this meeting for fun or business?" he asked as they fell into step next to each other and walked along the crushed stone path.

"Definitely not fun," she responded. Now that she was about to tell him about Luis, she was having second thoughts. It was tempting—so tempting—to pretend everything was okay. As long as she didn't update her blog, Luis shouldn't have any way to find her, and a childish part of her felt as though as long as she didn't talk about it, it wouldn't be real.

"Has someone else been attacked at the hotel?"

She shook her head. "Nothing like that. It's about Luis."

"Did he manage to contact you?" Samuel asked, looking worried.

She took a deep breath. "It's worse than that. He left Michigan. I think he's coming to find me himself."

Samuel's footsteps faltered. When she turned to look at him, he was staring at her, his eyes wide. "He's on his way here?"

"I don't know for sure. I heard the news second-hand, from a friend." She related her conversation with Leslie, then let him read the messages, in case he picked up something she had missed. He handed the phone back to her with a serious expression.

"This isn't good."

"I know."

They kept walking after a second. They were both silent for a few minutes, then Samuel, who must have been waiting for her to make the first move, ventured, "What are you going to do?"

"I'm planning on leaving," she said. "I don't know where I'm going to go yet, but I'm not going to update the blog or tell anyone where my new destination is." She hesitated. "Well, I'll tell my parents, and I'll tell you, but no one else. I don't want to chance it getting back to him. I want to go somewhere he won't expect, somewhere out of the way."

"I guess the good news is you aren't going to keep trying to solve the murder on your own anymore," he said, giving her a wry smile. "Out of one frying pan and into another seems to be your modus operandi."

"It's going to drive me crazy leaving without knowing who killed Trisha, but I'm willing to live with the mystery if it means staying away from Luis."

"Do you want me to help you?" he asked. "Whatever you need. I've dealt with stalkers before. I know how frightening they can be."

"I don't know what you could do," she admitted. "Short of being my full-time bodyguard, anyway. Unless you think you could get a bead on Luis? If I knew for a fact where he was, I would feel a lot better."

"Give me all of his information—his cell phone number, his license plate number, anything you can think of—and I'll see what I can do," he told her. He paused and so did she, turning to look at him. When he opened his arms, she stepped forward into the hug. "It's going to be all right. I can't promise he won't find you, but I can promise that if he does, I'll be right there to make sure he doesn't try anything."

It felt good to be held, and she rested her head against his shoulder for a long moment. "Thanks," she said when she finally pulled away. "I hate this. I hate having to be afraid of him. The sooner I leave, the better. I'm going to start packing when I get back to my room."

"Do you want me to come up with you?"

She hesitated, then shook her head. "Thanks for offering, but I'd rather you start looking for Luis. The hotel has security, so if I see him there, I'll be able to get help. Not knowing how close he is will drive me crazy. I need to know if he's still halfway across the country, or if he's already in San Francisco. It will give me peace of mind, if nothing else."

He nodded. "Understandable. I can't promise quick results, but I'll do my best."

"Thank you. Do whatever you need to do. And feel free to charge me for it. You know my financial situation—I'm willing to pay literally anything to know how close Luis is to me."

He gave her an odd look. "I'm not going to charge you a penny. This isn't a job to me, Tulia. I'm going to help you on my own time, no matter how long it takes." He cracked a grin. "Plus, I'm on vacation, and I'm pretty sure it goes against my contract with the agency to moonlight on my own."

She was touched. She hadn't wanted him to feel as though she was taking advantage of their friendship, but it was nice to know that he cared, that he really wanted to help her, not just make a few bucks.

"Well, thank you. I really appreciate it. You have no idea how good it feels to know I have at least one person in my corner."

They walked for a little while longer, circling through the park. She showed him Cicero's trick of flying to her, and he made a good suggestion, which was getting a heavy-duty kite string so Cicero could fly longer distances without worrying about getting lost.

Afterward, he walked her back to the hotel, where he watched as she went inside. Maybe she should have invited him up to her room, but she was already keeping her eyes peeled for Luis, and she knew that if she caused any commotion, the hotel staff would be right there to see what was going on. Everyone had been on high alert since the murder.

Her main reason for not wanting him to come up —so he could start looking for her ex right away— was true, but the other reason, the one she hadn't told him, had more to do with her own sense of independence. This trip had given her so much confidence in herself. She hated the thought of becoming dependent on someone now. She couldn't expect Samuel to be with her for every step of the rest of her trip, and she needed to learn to be comfortable on her own even knowing that Luis was out there.

For a second, she was tempted to go home, see if she could stay with her parents for a little while, and figure things out from there. She dismissed the thought quickly. She was going to finish this trip one way or another. If she did ever decide to end it early, it certainly wasn't going to be because of Luis.

CHAPTER TEN

Tulia crossed the hotel's entrance area quickly, Cicero clinging painfully to her shoulder with his claws. She reached up a hand to steady him, murmuring an apology. She didn't like being so exposed, knowing Luis could be watching her from somewhere.

There were already two men waiting for the elevator when she got there. She hung back for a second, but neither of them was Luis. In fact, she recognized them both—one was Callie's fiancé, and the other his best man. Chase and Cody, she thought their names were.

When the elevator arrived, the doors opening with a ding, she stepped forward with them, following them into the elevator. Chase held the doors for her politely, and then hit the button for their floor without asking her where she was going. She leaned against the railing in the back, petting Cicero's soft head gently.

Cody leaned against the same railing too close on the other side of her. She could smell alcohol on him, and had to force herself not to sidle away. Instead, she put a pleasant smile on her face and said, "How are you guys doing?"

"At this point, we are still trying to figure things out," Chase said. "Trisha's death has been hard on all of us, but especially on the women. Callie and Kasey have known Trisha for years. She was practically like another sister to them."

"Man, I can't believe she's gone," Cody said. "Her family is going to sue the crap out of this hotel. I'll bet you anything it was one of their employees who did it. They were probably stealing, and she caught them in the act. You can't trust the staff at places like this."

"That doesn't seem fair," Tulia said. "They all seem perfectly nice to me."

"Ignore Cody; he's a jerk," Chase said matter-of-factly.

His friend just rolled his eyes. "You say that like it's a bad thing. Women love it."

"That's why I'm getting married, and you're still single, huh?" Chase asked.

Cody snorted. "Better to be single and free than trapped with the wrong person. You tell me how your marriage is going a few months down the line, buddy."

Chase bristled. "What's that supposed to mean?"

"Nothing, I'm just saying. Your relationship isn't exactly off to an auspicious start."

"If you've got something to say, we can talk about it when we get back to the room," Chase said. He turned to Tulia. "Sorry. Like I said, what happened to Trisha has been hard on all of us."

The elevator arrived at their floor. When the door opened, Chase strode off first and unlocked the door to his and Cody's shared room. Cody hung back while Tulia searched through her own phone for the correct application.

"Do you have a best friend?"

She looked over at him, raising her eyebrows. He had definitely been drinking. "I'm not sure. It's been a weird couple of months."

"Well, that's sad." It took him a second to remember whatever he was going to say, then he said, "If you did, and they betrayed you, would you forgive them? If they apologized?"

"Depends on how bad it was," she said shortly, thinking of Luis. "But probably not. If I'm going to share a part of my life with someone, I'd want to be able to trust them. What's all this about?"

"Just trying to figure some stuff out," he mumbled. He glanced toward her door as she finally got it open. "You up for some company?"

"Thanks, but I'm good."

She quickly stepped through, shut the door in his face, and turned the deadbolt. She waited, but no knock came, and when she checked the peephole, he had already left the hallway, hopefully having gone into his own room with Chase. Maybe she had been a bit rude, but she didn't know him and wasn't about to trust someone who was on her list of possible murder suspects. Though, maybe she could have gotten something important from him if she'd kept him talking.

She hesitated for a second, her curiosity fighting with her desire to leave the area and do her best to avoid running into Luis. This time, common sense won, and she turned away from the door. After taking Cicero's harness off him, she put him down on top of his cage while she started packing. It felt weird not to be updating her blog about her next destination. She didn't even know what her next destination *was*. All she knew was that she wanted it to be far from here, someplace where Luis would have a hard time finding her.

She had gotten about half of her clothing back into her suitcase when something thudded against her hotel room door. The noise was eerily similar to the sound she had heard when Trisha was getting murdered, and she froze, her heart pounding in her chest.

The noise didn't come again, but now that she was focusing, she could hear raised voices in the hallway. She walked across the suite and looked out the peephole. There was a small group of people standing in the hall, arguing. She saw Callie and Kasey, along with the assistant manager, Miles, and someone else who looked like he was on the hotel staff. Callie was restraining Kasey, holding onto her arm as Kasey pulled toward Miles, who was rubbing his shoulder. Worried, Tulia unlocked the door and pulled it open.

"What's going on?" she asked, coming half out of her room.

The hotel staff member she hadn't recognized turned toward her, and she saw the manager tag on his shirt. He was the same man she had seen talking to the police the day before.

"Not to worry, ma'am. The situation is being handled."

"He killed Trisha," Kasey said. "And he just tried to break into our room, probably to finish us off!"

"I was coming to check in on you," Miles said, crossing his arms. "It was a courtesy call. You are the one who got physical with me. I'm not comfortable working with guests who get violent."

"There was no cause to shove him, Kasey," Callie said to her sister. "Sorry, Tulia. That's probably what disturbed you. She pushed Miles against your door."

"He's the one Trisha got into an argument with the day she died," Kasey said. "I can't believe he's still working here. He even still has access to our rooms."

"Can everyone please just take a deep breath?" the manager said. His name tag labeled him as Burt. "Ma'am, it's against our policy to allow any violence towards our staff."

"He came into my room without even knocking. One of my best friends was just murdered, and the person who did it is still out there. He's lucky I didn't do worse."

Burt turned to his employee, frowning. "Is this true, Miles? Did you enter their room?"

"The door was unlocked. I knocked, and it swung partially open. I didn't cross the threshold."

"I was afraid for my life," Kasey said. "How can you let him keep working here?"

"I will handle it, miss," Bert said. "Please do not physically engage any of my staff members. If there's a problem in the future, come find me. For now, I'll ensure that you don't run into Miles again."

"Come on, Kasey," Callie said. "That's as good as it's going to get. Let's go back into the room and cool off."

They left, going into the room next to Tulia's. Tulia retreated into her own room, but stayed close to the door, listening.

"I'm sorry, Miles," Bert said. "This isn't the first guest who has complained about you since the incident. I'm going to put you on temporary leave while the police finish investigating what happened."

"Paid leave?" Miles asked, his voice tight.

"You know we don't do that," Bert said, sounding regretful. Tulia looked out the peephole in time to see him clap a hand on Miles's shoulder. "Just look at it as an unexpected vacation. Assuming the police don't find anything, you'll be back to your regular job in no time. And if you remember anything about what happened to that security footage, give me a call. I'm on your side, son, understood?"

Miles didn't respond as he jerked away from

Burt's touch and strode down the hallway. Burt ran a hand through his hair, the expression on his face one of intense stress. After a moment, he walked away as well, leaving the hallway empty.

CHAPTER ELEVEN

Hoping she wouldn't have any more disturbances, Tulia returned to her suitcase and continued packing. While she worked, she thought about where to go next. She had a general idea of the direction she wanted to head in, but wasn't sure if she wanted to find an actual attraction, or just strike out and drive for a few hours, then stop at whatever town she happened to be near when she was ready for a break.

Unless Luis had somehow managed to put a physical tracking device on her or her RV, he shouldn't be able to find her location as long as she didn't put it on her blog. She was still kicking herself for not being more careful with that. She had known he was looking for her, but she'd never once dreamed he would actually strike out on his own in search of her.

If anything, she had been half waiting for a notification that he was suing her. She was relatively certain he didn't have any legal claim to her money, and she'd been willing and ready to fight back against him in court.

She only managed to get a few more articles of clothing in before someone knocked at the door. Biting back a sound of irritation, she tossed the shirt she was holding into her suitcase and strode over to the door, peering out the peephole. She opened it to Kasey.

"Sorry to bother you," the other woman said. "But we need to talk to you."

Tulia hesitated, wanting nothing more than to tell her she didn't have time. She had made the decision to leave, and now she wanted to do it. But Kasey looked dead serious, and Tulia reminded herself that she had lost a friend. She could take some time to listen to whatever she and Callie had to say.

"All right, just let me grab my phone," she said.

A moment later, she was walking into the neighboring hotel room. This one was a bit neater than the one Trisha had been killed in—the women hadn't unpacked anything and certainly hadn't been spending their evenings partying. Callie was sitting on the couch, her hair pulled back into a simple ponytail, her eyes red rimmed. She had her legs tucked up and her arms around her knees.

"Listen, I know you're probably already more involved in this than you want to be," Kasey said as soon as the door shut behind them. Tulia noticed they had engaged the deadbolt so the hotel door wouldn't swing all the way shut. She knew some people did that to keep from getting locked out of their rooms, but it didn't seem like the best practice when there was a killer on the loose.

"I'm not going to deny that I wish none of this had happened, but if I can do something to help, I want to," she said. "What's going on?"

"No one believes me," Kasey said. She gestured at Callie, who didn't say anything or respond at all. "Even Callie doesn't. I know it was Miles. It has to be him. If you look at it logically, everything fits. Trisha got into a big argument with him earlier that day in front of a lot of people. He's the assistant manager—no matter what anyone else says, he must've had a way to access the security footage. He would have had a key, and none of the guests or staff would have thought twice about the assistant manager walking around. Even if someone did spot him walking to the room, they probably wouldn't have registered him. People in uniforms are practically invisible. I *know* he did it, I just need evidence, something that will get the police to stop dragging their feet. You were right there, in the room next to ours. You had to have heard something or seen something. I just want my friend to get justice, Tulia. Can you try to remember if there is anything at all that you might have skipped over or forgotten to mention to the police?"

Tulia held back on her first urge to claim she didn't remember anything and really *thought* about it. She hadn't been paying much attention when the attack happened; she remembered the thuds, but that was because they stood out to her. Was it possible she had missed the sound of voices, or even something as innocuous as a door opening and closing?

Completely. She was used to staying in motels with paper thin walls on the rare occasion she took a trip somewhere; the sound of other guests was something she would have simply tuned out. Biting her lip, she tried to put herself back in the moment; she had been sipping her wine, watching the television, and relaxing. Nothing had been bothering her; she hadn't been keeping half an ear on raised voices in the other room. All she remembered was hearing the first thud, deciding it was nothing, then hearing the second one a moment later and being marginally more worried. It wasn't until she heard Callie's crying that she realized something was really wrong.

"Nothing," she said after racking her memory. "I'm sorry. I wish I could say I heard voices or a shout or something, but I didn't."

"You saw the argument, right?" Kasey asked. "I remember, you were there."

"I was, but I don't know if that means he killed her," Tulia said. "He seems like the obvious suspect, like you said; if the police haven't arrested him, they must have good reason. He must have an alibi."

Kasey moaned, sitting down on the couch next to her sister. "I don't know what to do. No one saw anything. No one knows anything. We've been spending day after day at the police station, answering questions and looking for answers. Callie was supposed to get married tomorrow. Now we're stuck in this never-ending limbo. I'm *so sure* it was that assistant manager, but no one is listening to me."

Tulia looked toward Callie, who had been sitting quietly, staring off into the distance the whole time. Trisha's death seemed to be affecting both of them differently, but equally as severely. She thought about Cody, who seemed to constantly be drinking, and knew it wasn't just the women who were upset. They had all been friends, had all been close. Chase seemed to be the only one who was handling it somewhat well.

Before she could think of something to say, though she wasn't sure she could come up with something comforting even if she tried, someone knocked brusquely on the door. Kasey got up to answer it, Tulia staring curiously after her. The other woman opened the door to Chase and Cody. Cody stumbled past Kasey to sit heavily on a chair, and Chase cleared his throat.

"Can we come in?" His words were directed to his fiancé. Callie didn't meet his gaze; she just shrugged. Chase seemed to take that as an invitation, because he stepped past the threshold. Tulia realized she hadn't seen them together since the day of Trisha's death, and wondered just how hard the murder had been on their relationship.

"Um, just so you know, one of the hotel staff is waiting outside your room," Chase said to her as he passed by, going to sit next to Callie. He took a spot on the opposite end of the couch from her, seeming strangely hesitant.

Tulia blinked. What could one of the hotel staff want with her? She hadn't told them she was checking out yet. Maybe Luis had shown up and started asking for her. The thought set off a coil of tension in her stomach.

"I'd better go. Sorry I wasn't more help," she said, directing her words to Kasey. The other woman's lips pressed together.

"I'm starting to think this whole situation's beyond help. Thanks for trying, though."

Tulia left the room full of broken people behind, letting the door swing shut behind her—the deadbolt was still in place, keeping the door from latching—and turned her head to see the very man Kasey was so convinced was a killer standing right in front of her room. Miles looked at her, the assistant manager tag already gone. He held his hand out to her, and she looked down at it. He was holding a small SD card.

"I'm done with this place," he said. "My boss, the guests, all of it. Maybe I should take this to the police, but frankly, I'm done with them too. Do whatever you want with it."

"What—" she began.

"It's the missing security footage." He dumped the SD card in her hand.

"Why me?"

She was half expecting him to say something like he had read her blog, or he was giving it to her because she'd been polite after the big blowup with Trisha. He just shrugged and said, "I heard you talking to that guy, the one you met for lunch. Sounds like he's a PI or something. I figure he'd be the sort of person who knows what to do with it. I'd rather one of you watches it first, because I'd rather not get in trouble if this doesn't even contain any clues about the murder."

He gave her a short wave and turned, striding toward the elevator. She gaped after him. In the neighboring room, she heard raised voices, and hurriedly got out her phone to unlock her door.

She didn't know what secrets were hiding on the missing footage, but somehow she didn't think it was going to contain proof that Miles had murdered Trisha. As far as she was concerned, her suspect list had just gotten one shorter—and the remainder of the suspects were in the room right next to hers.

CHAPTER TWELVE

The first thing she did after locking the door was sit down at the table with the SD card in front of her and call Samuel. He answered with an apology.

"I'm still working on tracking him down. Sorry, I don't have any results yet."

"It's not that," she said, not worried about Luis for once. She might have the tools to solve a murder at her fingertips. "The hotel's assistant manager just quit and left me with an SD card he says contains the missing security footage."

"He's the one who got into an argument with her, right? Have you contacted the police yet?"

"He said he wanted us to watch it first. Something about how he didn't want to get in trouble if it didn't contain anything useful. He didn't really elaborate."

"Why'd he take the footage if he doesn't know what's on it?" She could hear the frown in his voice.

"I have no idea. It doesn't make any sense to me either, but I'm starting to think he probably didn't kill Trisha."

"Unless this is his way of confessing," Samuel suggested. "What do you want to do with it?"

"That's why I'm calling you. I don't think I should be the one to decide."

"He gave it to you."

"Only because he overheard that you were a private investigator."

Samuel fell silent for a second, then said, "I'll come over and get it. We can pop it in, see if it's even the right footage. I think we should give it to the police regardless of whether it seems to contain anything incriminating, though. We don't want to withhold evidence."

"Right." She stared down at the SD card. "You'll be here soon?"

"Twenty minutes at most."

"Okay. Thanks, Samuel. See you soon."

She hung up as soon as he said goodbye, still staring at the SD card. Through the hotel room wall, she could hear raised voices; she couldn't make out what they were saying, but none of the four of them sounded happy. Had one of them killed Trisha? She didn't know, but she knew how to find out.

She should wait for Samuel. She told herself that even as she unlocked her laptop, slid the SD card into the reader, and waited for the files to load.

There were ten different folders on the SD card, each labelled with a different code. Some didn't make sense right off the bat, but FrntDsk was obvious. She opened the folder and found a series of video files, each one half an hour long.

She was beginning to realize that there was a *lot* of footage to go through. More than she would be able to look through on her own before Samuel arrived.

Still, she wanted to try. First, she wanted to find out what Miles was hiding. She opened the first video file, which was earlier in the evening and saw Miles behind the front desk. She fast-forwarded through it, watching as he talked to person after person. Nothing else happened, so she went to the next video file.

Halfway through this one, Miles received a call and left the desk when it ended. At first, she was excited that something was happening, then realized her problem. She had no idea where he was going. She noted the time he left the frame on her phone, then returned to the list of different folders on the SD card. There was FrntDsk, H1-201-210, H1-211-220 and so on, up to H3-311-320. Then there was DB, Dining, Entr, and Pool. She opened Entr and saw the entrance area, opposite the front desk. Pool was self-explanatory, and she figured Dining was the room with the complimentary breakfast. DB was a mystery, so she clicked that and then loaded up the file that should coincide with Mile's disappearance from the front desk camera. DB, it turned out, must have stood for Delivery Bay, because it showed a back entrance to the hotel with a big delivery door, a smaller door for people, and next to it, a dumpster. She fast-forwarded until she saw a windowless van drive up. Nothing happened right away, so she fast-forwarded more until she saw the door to the hotel open.

Miles came out. An older man got out of the van and helped him unload a trolly with laundry in dry-cleaning bags hanging up on it. Once he was done, the man got back into the van and drove away. Mile stood there, staring at the trolly. After a second, he started looking through the clothes, reading the tags. He selected a handful of items, glanced around, then walked toward the dumpster, opening it up and tossing the laundry in.

After another look around, he started pushing the trolly inside. When he was standing in the doorframe, he paused and looked directly up at the camera. Then, he went inside.

Tulia blinked, both surprised and not surprised by what she had just seen. It seemed that, after the argument with Trisha, he hadn't been in a forgiving mood. She would bet a good amount of her lottery winnings that the clothing items he had thrown away were the very ones she had started yelling at him over. She got it—she had worked in customer service, and while she'd never done anything like that, she'd be lying if she said she hadn't been tempted.

It was evident by the look on his face when he looked up at the camera that he had forgotten it was there. *That explains why he stole the SD card,* she thought. He hadn't wanted his actions to be caught on camera. It wasn't an innocent reason, but it also wasn't exactly murder.

She was more sure than ever he hadn't killed Trisha—he had already gotten his revenge, after all, petty as it might have been. But that didn't explain who had.

She returned to the main screen, opening the folder for the hallway her original room had been on —H3-301-310. Biting her lip, she thought back, trying to remember when the attack had occurred. She opened the file she thought was the right one and watched, fast-forwarding through it with her finger on the space bar, ready to pause if she saw someone.

Other than one family returning to their room right at the very beginning of it, and until the end when she saw herself come out of her own room, the hallway remained empty. The file ended just as Kasey opened the door.

Frowning, Tulia opened the file for the previous half hour. She fast-forwarded through the whole thing, but only saw Kasey, Trisha, and Callie go into the room at the beginning of it. A few minutes later, Kasey left. No one else entered the room; no one even paused in front of the door. Cody walked by once, but just to go into his own room, and she didn't see Chase.

Feeling like she was missing something, Tulia went through the footage again. How could Trisha have been murdered if no one went into the room?

"Oh," she whispered, watching the footage of the three women, happy and smiling, walking into their room together. "I see."

She knew who killed Trisha. It wasn't about who had entered the room, but rather who had left it. Or, who hadn't.

CHAPTER THIRTEEN

The argument was still going on next door as Tulia ejected the SD card and put it on the table in front of her closed laptop. She checked her phone for the time; it had been about fifteen minutes since she had gotten off the phone with Samuel, which meant he should be there soon.

She felt antsy. She didn't know what to do with the knowledge she had. Her eyes seemed drawn to the SD card, the knowledge of what was on it tempting her to watch more of the files, just to make sure she hadn't missed anything. She didn't want to risk it, though. The police would need this as evidence; she had no doubt about that now. She couldn't risk accidentally corrupting a file or damaging the card.

She tried to just sit there and wait, but the

shouting next door was just getting louder. The group of friends, previously five and now four, seemed to be imploding in on itself. Maybe this had been building for days, ever since Trisha's death, or even longer. She didn't know. She didn't even know *why* the person who had murdered Trisha had killed her. It made her sad to think about the feeling of betrayal Trisha must have had, mixed in with her fear and pain. Tulia knew how much it hurt when someone you were close to broke your trust.

Something thudded against the wall in an eerie echo of what she had heard during the attack on Trisha. Tulia jumped up, her heart in her throat. She heard more shouting, and wished she could make out the words.

Samuel would be here soon. She knew she shouldn't get involved. Even as she fished her pepper spray out of her purse, she told herself going over there was a bad idea.

But that's what I told myself when Trisha was being attacked, her conscience told her. *I might have been able to save her if I tried.*

Armed with only the truth and her pepper spray, she shoved her phone into her back pocket, told Cicero to be good, and left her hotel room. The door to the neighboring room was still slightly open, since the deadbolt was keeping it from latching. The shouting had subsided for the moment, but Tulia had already made up her mind. She knocked lightly on the door and pushed it open, not waiting for a response.

All four of them turned to look at her. Cody was standing against the wall that bordered their two rooms, his hands up in surrender. There was a hole in the wall next to his head—probably what Tulia had heard just moments before. Chase was standing nearby, shaking out his hand. His knuckles were split.

Across the room, Kasey had her arms around her sister's shoulders, and Callie's face was streaked with tears.

"Sorry," Kasey said, her tone muted. "We didn't mean to disturb you. We'll be quieter."

"Will we?" Chase snapped. "I don't exactly feel like keeping my voice down. I just found out my *fiancé* has been cheating on me with my *best friend*."

Tulia's head snapped back around to Cody. That had to be motive for murder, but she still wasn't sure how Trisha fit. "Dude, I told you I was sorry," Cody said. "I know I shouldn't have—she came on to me. I was going to end it before the wedding."

"This isn't like the time you broke my CD player back in elementary school," Chase snapped. "You can't just say sorry and get out of it. We're done. I'm done with all of you. In case you need me to spell it out for you, Callie, the wedding is off. I'd say I hope you can get some of your deposits back, but I really don't care."

"No, please—" Callie began, but Chase cut her off.

"I am a forgiving person, but this crosses the line. I don't need to hear excuses, because there *is* no excuse. And you." He rounded on Cody who shrunk back. "I guess I owe you a thanks for telling me, but don't think that means I'm ever going to forgive you. I just need to know one thing."

"What?" Cody asked, his eyes wide.

"Did you kill her?"

Cody blinked. "Who?"

"Trisha," Chase snapped. "She told me she wanted to talk to me, just a few hours before she died. She was going to tell me, wasn't she? You must have found out and wanted to keep it quiet."

"I didn't kill her, man," Cody said. "I swear."

Finally, it all clicked for Tulia. She knew not only who the killer was, but the motive behind it. Before Chase could say anything, she spoke up.

"He's telling the truth. He didn't do it."

Chase turned on her, some of his anger turning to confusion. "How do you know? Did you do it?"

She gave him a flat look. Maybe she should have expected the accusation to come earlier; as far as they knew, she had been right next door the whole time leading up to Trisha's death. She could have popped over, done the deed, and been back in her room before anyone was the wiser.

"No," she said, turning to raise her finger. "It was her."

"Callie?" Chase stared at his fiancé—ex-fiancé— as she sank back into her sister's arms. Kasey turned her head to stare at her, then looked back up at Tulia, her gaze narrowing.

"You'd better have some proof to back up that accusation. Callie's been a shell of herself since Trisha died."

"I have proof," Tulia said. She swallowed, suddenly nervous. She was glad she had left the SD card in her room, which was locked. "That assistant manager, Miles, he gave me the missing security footage. I watched the footage of the hallway our old rooms were in, and didn't see anyone but Kasey, Callie, and Trisha go into their room. And only Kasey left the room before Trisha was killed."

"That's not evidence," Kasey said, angry. "That's just … a guess. It's circumstantial. Plus, you must be missing something. Callie was at the gym. Right, Callie?"

She turned to her sister, who drew away, backing toward the suite's bedroom. She shook her head. "I-I don't know."

"What do you mean, you don't know? You told me you just got back from the gym and found her like that."

"I meant to go to the gym," Callie said, her voice shaking. "But she told me … she gave me an ultimatum. I don't know how she learned about the affair with Cody, but she told me either I had to tell Chase before the wedding or she would. She didn't listen when I told her Cody and I had agreed to end it before the wedding. We … we fought. I pushed her. She fell into the wall and came back at me, trying to slap me. I pushed her again, but that time she fell and hit her head on the table going down."

Kasey backed away from her sister, staring at her with shock painted across her face. Behind Tulia, Cody groaned. She turned to see him slide down the wall with his head in his hands.

"Callie, you…?"

"Then you went and told him anyway," Callie snapped, rounding on Cody. "You wrecked *everything.*"

"At least he had the decency to feel guilty about what he did," Chase said. "He might have been months late to the draw, but he did tell me, Callie. Were you ever going to tell me about you and Cody? What about what you did to Trisha? Were you going to keep that secret our entire marriage?"

"It wasn't my fault," Callie said, blinking tears out of her eyes. "I felt horrible. The instant I realized what happened, I wished I could take it back. But it was too late. If I could rewind time, I would, but I can't. Why should I have wrecked my entire life for a mistake?"

"Because it would have been the right thing to do," Kasey said, staring at her sister like she had never seen her before. "I suspected something was going on between you and Cody, and I should have confronted you sooner, but I kept telling myself you were a good person. That it wasn't what I thought it was. I never questioned it when you said you'd been at the gym and just got back to the room. I don't even know who you are anymore, Callie."

"I'm going to call the police," Chase said. He gave Callie a long look. "We were supposed to get married tomorrow. Some wedding this is, huh?"

He turned away, reaching into his pocket for his phone. Before he could dial, there was a light knock at the door. Tulia looked up to see Samuel push it open. He took in the scene, then his eyes met hers. He raised an eyebrow.

"You watched the footage from the SD card, didn't you?"

"Well," she said, a little embarrassed but mostly glad to see him. "It's not as if you wouldn't have."

"You've got me there."

EPILOGUE

Despite her best efforts, Tulia ended up staying at the hotel for another night. It took ages to go down to the police station and give her statement. Samuel drove her, and his company was a welcome distraction, though he kept teasing her about watching the footage without him.

"If you had been given Pandora's box, you wouldn't have lasted ten minutes, would you?" he said as they got back into his car once the police were finally done taking in her convoluted story. They had already surrendered the SD card. She hoped Miles didn't get into any sort of trouble for throwing away the clothing Trisha had yelled at him about. It might have been petty, but he'd done the right thing in the end.

"Of course not," she replied as she buckled her seatbelt. "Who gives someone a box, tells them not to open it, and expects them to actually listen?"

"No wonder humanity is doomed," he said with a dramatic sigh. "We're cursed with curiosity; the most dangerous force in the universe."

"Speaking of curiosity," she said as he pulled out onto the road. "I'm leaving tomorrow, but I want to try to salvage this stop. San Francisco seems like a cool city, and I've barely seen any of it. Do you want to drive across the Golden Gate Bridge with me before heading back to the hotel?"

"You didn't cross it on your way in?"

"No, the lot I left my RV in is to the south of the city. It would have been out of my way."

"Then your wish is my command. Let's go be tourists."

She was glad it was a clear day, because the view as they approached the bridge was impressive. It was the color, mostly; it stood out against the skyline, vibrant and proud. She paid the toll, giving Samuel a glare when he tried to object, and snapped a picture as they crossed it.

On the other side, they turned around and did it again, since her hotel was back across the bay.

"What do you think?" he asked as they drove back across.

She bit her lip. "Honestly ... it's a little disappointing." He gave her a disbelieving look, and she explained, "It's just that the Mackinac Bridge is longer, okay? I'm from Michigan. Everyone knows we have the best bridge. The Golden Gate Bridge is a cool color, I'll give it that, but seriously, over nine dollars for a toll? That's more than twice the cost of the Mackinac Bridge's toll, but for less than half the length." She sniffed. "I feel cheated."

He started laughing, and she rolled her eyes. "I didn't expect you to be so biased."

"Michigan is my home," she said, feeling a surge of homesickness. "I'm allowed a little bias."

"There's nothing wrong with that." He turned toward her hotel. "Where are you going next?"

"Southeast," she said. "I'm not sure exactly where yet. I'm going to finish packing when I get back to my room, then go get my RV and head out. I'll drive until I'm tired, then see what's interesting nearby. I'm not going to post about it, though. Not for a while."

"You'll let me know if you stop off somewhere for a few days?"

She nodded. "Of course. What are you going to do?"

"I'm going to stick around here for a few days and keep my eyes peeled for Luis. If he shows up, you'll be the first to know. You might want to pretend you're still in the hotel; it will be a good trap for him."

"Good idea." She smiled over at Samuel. "Thanks. Again. For everything. I feel like I've been saying that a lot."

"No thanks are necessary. We'll find him before he finds you. That's all there is to it."

She tried to take his words to heart as she looked out the window at the city passing them by. She wouldn't feel completely safe until she knew for a fact where Luis was, but the thought of being on the road again felt good. She might not be going back to Michigan quite yet, but the RV had become a home to her, and she missed it.

Made in the USA
Coppell, TX
12 October 2023

22758504R00066